STAYING

HEALTHY

CARE FOR YOUR BODY

Rhoda Nottridge

CRESTWOOD HOUSE
New York

STAYING HEALTHY

BE POSITIVE
CARE FOR YOUR BODY
EAT WELL
KEEP FIT

Series editor: Kathryn Smith
Series designer: Helen White

First published in the United States in 1993 by
Crestwood House
Macmillan Publishing Company
866 Third Avenue
New York, NY 10022

Macmillan Publishing Company is part of the Maxwell
Communication Group of Companies.

First Edition
Printed in Italy by G. Canale & C.S.p.A., Turin
10 9 8 7 6 5 4 3 2 1

Library of Congress Cataloging-in-Publication Data

Nottridge, Rhoda
      Care for your body / Rhoda Nottridge.—1st Ed.
         p. cm.—(Staying Healthy)
      Includes index.
      Summary: A guide to help teens understand and care for their
   changing body.
      ISBN 0-89686-787-0
      1. Teenagers—Health and hygiene—Juvenile literature.
   2. Adolescence—Juvenile literature.   3. Puberty—Juvenile
   literature. [1. Puberty.   2. Adolescence.   3. Health.]   I. Title.
   II. Series.
   RA777.N67   1993
   613'.0433—dc20
                                          92-13917

CONTENTS

A HEAD START   **4**

KEEPING CLEAN   **12**

BODY CHOICES   **17**

BODY ABUSE   **25**

BODY HELP   **28**

GLOSSARY   **30**

BOOKS TO READ   **31**

FURTHER INFORMATION   **31**

INDEX   **32**

A HEAD START

Learning to look after yourself

When you were a young child, your parents or whoever brought you up looked after you. They made sure that you had enough to eat. They kept you clean, they took care of you when you were ill, and they tried to stop you from hurting yourself.

As you grow up, one of the most important responsibilities you develop is learning to look after yourself. When you are an adult, no one is going to look after your body for you, so you have to look after it for yourself.

As your body changes, you enter an exciting new period in your life. To make the most of your changing body, it helps if you find out about ways to stay healthy—and hazards to avoid. Caring for your body starts as soon as you want it to. It's worth starting right away, because after all, your body has to last a lifetime!

Changing times

Your body goes through all kinds of changes as you grow up. You get taller and your shape changes in other ways. Girls develop wider hips and their breasts begin to grow. Boys get bigger muscles and their shoulders become broader. Even your face changes shape! The nose and jaw become more prominent and your hairline begins to recede.

▶ Learning to look after yourself is an important part of growing up.

▼ As you grow up, your body changes in many ways. Even the shape of your face will become different.

▲ If you find out which skin type you have, it will help you know how to clean your skin properly and keep it looking healthy.

▶ BELOW RIGHT Although acne can be upsetting, there are steps you can take to improve the condition. Consult your doctor for advice.

Recognizing your skin type

There are three main skin types:

Dry

Dry skin can look flaky and feel tight after washing with soap and water. It may become rough in cold weather because not enough sebum is produced. If washing with soap and water dries the skin out too much, using a cream cleanser may help. Moisturizers put a film over surface skin, which helps keep moisture in. If your skin is dry all over your body, try putting a little unperfumed baby oil in your bathwater.

Skin deep

Skin keeps your body waterproof and stops infections getting inside you. Your skin has two layers. The surface skin is called the epidermis. This top layer of skin is dead and is constantly being worn away and replaced. The layer under this is called the dermis. The roots of your hair are in the dermis, along with the sebaceous and sweat glands.

When you get hot, your sweat glands send waste out through your pores to cool you down. Pores are tiny openings in the skin. The sebaceous glands produce an oily substance called sebum, which stops your skin from drying out and helps to keep it waterproof.

Skin problems

During adolescence, changes in the levels of sex hormones in the body can lead to an increase in the amount of sebum that your body produces. It is a buildup of sebum that can cause pimples.

Blackheads are caused when there is too much sebum and when a pore is blocked by dead skin on the surface. The black color is caused by the dead skin coming into contact with oxygen in the air.

Whiteheads are small spots caused when the sebaceous or sweat glands become blocked. The sebum hardens in the blocked pores.

Sometimes a blockage of a pore in a sebaceous gland makes the gland burst. The skin around the spot becomes infected and inflamed. Acne is an area of skin with lots of these spots and is common among teenagers.

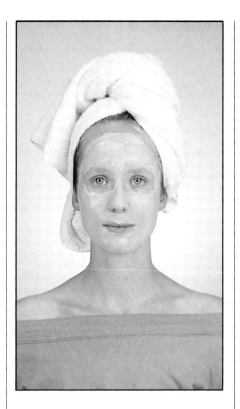

Oily

On oily skin the pores are sometimes visible and the skin looks shiny. Too much sebum is produced and the pores tend to attract dirt, making the skin prone to pimples. The skin should be washed with soap and water or a nongreasy cleanser. It is best not to scrub hard at the skin, as this may make the sebaceous glands produce more sebum. Astringents can be used to remove some oil and dirt.

Combination

This is the most common skin type. It means that you have dry areas around the cheeks, eyes and throat and an oily panel across the forehead, nose and chin. The skin needs to be treated in two ways, moisturizing the dry patches and cleaning the oily panels as with the above routine.

Six stoppers

It may not be possible to stop pimples from forming, but there are some ways in which it might be possible to stop them spreading further.

• Try to avoid fried or greasy foods, as these increase the amount of sebum that the skin produces.

• Eat plenty of fresh fruit, green vegetables, milk, eggs, potatoes, carrots and cereals. These provide vitamins C,D and E. Your body needs these to make and keep healthy skin.

• You can lose over four quarts of water through your skin on a hot day. Help to replace this by drinking plenty of water.

• Wash your skin regularly using mild or unperfumed soap and water. Make sure that towels and washcloths are clean.

• Try to avoid squeezing or playing with pimples—even minute amounts of dirt from hands can cause or spread infection.

If a pimple has been squeezed, dab it gently with an antiseptic.

• A doctor may be able to prescribe creams or drugs to help with very bad acne. There are no miracle cures, but it is possible to control the condition a little. Acne tends to disappear anyway as teenagers grow up.

▲ TOP LEFT
A face mask can be used occasionally to remove dead surface skin, temporarily tighten the pores and freshen your face.

▲ TOP RIGHT
Sunshine can help to dry out pimples. However, it is important to protect your skin from the damaging ultraviolet rays of the sun with protective lotion.

◄ On a hot day, your skin sweats to help you cool down. You need to replace this by drinking plenty of water.

Sun and skin

A little bit of sunlight can do skin a lot of good and can even help clear up pimples. Through the action of sunlight on the skin we absorb vitamin D, which is essential for good health. People with dark skin absorb less sunlight through their skins, so if they live in countries without much sunlight they may need to take a vitamin D supplement, such as cod-liver oil.

People with white skin may want to get a suntan. However, the ultraviolet rays in sunlight harm the skin. They can burn the skin and eventually cause it to age easily. Skin cancer is also caused by too much suntanning. Apart from being sensible about not staying too long in the sun in order to avoid sunstroke, it is well worth using sun screens and working out which sun protection factor your skin needs. A slight tan gained slowly is better for the skin than a deep tan. People with dark or black skin have more protection against burning.

Hair help

Clean, well-kept hair helps you look and feel better. Like your skin, your hair is affected by the hormonal changes that your body goes through during adolescence. To keep your hair healthy and glossy, make sure you eat plenty of fresh fruit and vegetables.

Hair hassles
Oily hair

Wash frequently with mild shampoo. There are many mild shampoos specially designed for oily hair. Avoid brushing and touching the scalp, because this stimulates the glands that produce oil.

Dry hair

Wash about every four days. Avoid combing when wet, as this splits hairs.

Dandruff

This happens when scales of skin —which we lose all the time—pile up together and get trapped in the hair. Rinsing out shampoo properly helps prevent dandruff. Antidandruff preparations may also help.

◀ It is important to have your hair cut regularly. This not only keeps it in good condition but stimulates new hair growth.

Split ends and damaged hair

Get hair trimmed frequently and try not to brush hair roughly or dry it out with a very hot hair dryer. Bleaches and permanents all damage the hair; body waves and vegetable dyes are less harmful. Elastic bands will break your hair.

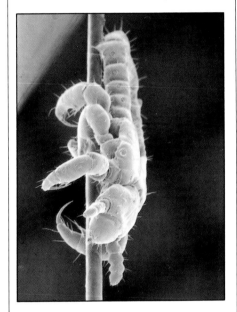

▲ This head louse has been magnified using an electron micrograph. These creatures inhabit the hair of the head, gluing their eggs to the scalp.

▶ LEFT Shaving opens up the pores on your face. After shaving, you need to splash cold water on your face to close them up and prevent dirt from getting in.

Lice

You can get head lice no matter how clean you and your hair are. Lice are tiny insects that lay eggs (called nits). These stick to the scalp and make your head itch. Check your hair regularly for signs of their little white eggs. Lotions that will get rid of them are available in drugstores. If someone in your family or a friend gets lice, you should check your hair carefully, as they are very easy to catch.

Body hair

Throughout your teenage years, your sex hormones become active. This encourages body hair growth. Both boys and girls may notice that their arms, legs and faces become more hairy. This is entirely normal. You will also grow hair under your arms and around the genitals.

Many women choose to remove hair from their legs or underarms. There is no medical reason for doing this. Shaving hair coarsens new hair growth, so it is important to think carefully about what you are doing before developing the habit of shaving off body hair.

Using hot-wax products can create broken veins on the legs and is best done only by a professional. Depilatory creams work well to remove hair if instructions are followed carefully. Special cream hair bleaches can be used to make dark hairs less noticeable.

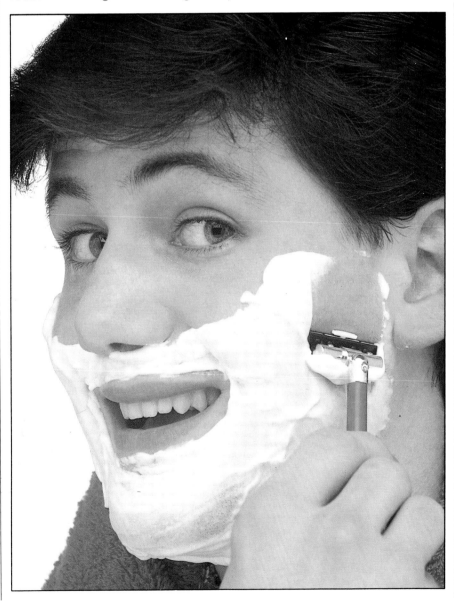

One of the last body changes that affects boys is the growth of a beard. If you decide to shave, there are many different types of electric razors or you can use foam and warm water and a disposable razor. This way of shaving cuts off the hairs closest to the skin. Warm water opens up the pores of the skin, so after shaving splash the skin with cold water to close them up again. This will prevent dirt from getting into the pores and causing pimples.

Eye problems
It is best to see a doctor immediately if you have any eye problems such as red, sticky, watery or inflamed eyes. These could be signs of infections such as conjunctivitis, or if eyes are red rimmed, blepharitis. Sties are caused when an eyelash becomes infected. Dabbing warm water on the eye with clean cotton may be soothing.

Eating carrots really does help people see in the dark. Carrots contain vitamin A, which helps your eyes work better, particularly in making out shapes of objects in poor light. If you can see

absolutely nothing in the dark, you may be lacking vitamin A in your diet.

◀ Glasses can be a great fashion accessory. There are a wide range of shapes and colors of frames available.

Color blindness
Color blindness means not being able to tell the difference between two colors, often red and green. Boys are more likely to be color-blind than girls. It is a condition that is inherited from your parents. It does not mean that you generally have difficulty seeing things. There are, however, some jobs that involve distinguishing different colors, and you may have difficulty with these. If you are color-blind, it may also be a good idea to take a friend with you when you buy clothes, to make sure that the colors match!

If you can see the number 29, you have normal sight.

If you mix up green and red, you will see the number 70.

Tired eyes
Some ways to be kind to your eyes:

Blink several times to wash your eyes with tears.

Rest your elbows on a table and cup your hands over your open eyes for a few minutes. Put tea bags, which have been soaked in cold water and squeezed out, onto closed eyes to soothe them.

Place a slice of cucumber on each closed eye.

Eye spy
Test your sight:

1. Covering each eye in turn, try to read a phone book about 20 inches away.

2. Then try to read a license plate number about 9 inches away.

If you have difficulty reading these clearly or suffer from frequent headaches, it may be worth having your eyes tested properly by an ophthalmologist. Many vision problems can be improved by the use of glasses or contact lenses. The Visual Therapy Approach is an alternative to this and involves relearning to use weakened eye muscles to try to improve some vision problems.

Ear piercing

If you want to get your ears pierced, make sure it is done only by a qualified jeweler who uses hygienic equipment This will keep infections from being passed on to you through reused equipment.

Pierced ears need to be kept very clean. Initially, wash both sides of the lobes at least once a day with soap and water and then dab them with rubbing alcohol.

Winning grins

Keeping teeth healthy will prevent problems in later years. It also adds to your looks and prevents bad breath.

Brushing routine

To prevent decay, you need to make sure you brush your teeth properly; otherwise, food will build up at the base of the teeth into a substance called plaque. This can cause decay and gum disease.

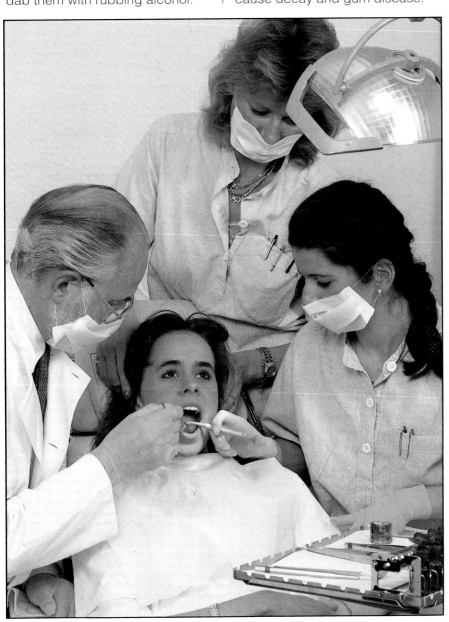

◀ A visit to the dentist every six months can help prevent tooth decay from getting worse.

▲ Regular brushing and flossing of teeth sweetens your breath and protects your teeth from decay.

Crooked teeth can be straightened by the dentist by temporarily fitting braces or a bite plate to your teeth.

Teeth tips

Brush teeth carefully at least twice a day or after meals and learn to use dental floss. Gently pull it up and down between your teeth to rub away plaque.

Try to avoid eating sugar and candy as these stick to the teeth, causing plaque and then decay.

Visit the dentist every six months to get your teeth checked and to have any plaque removed.

Change your toothbrush every three months.

To check teeth for plaque, you can buy a product called a discloser. This shows up plaque on your teeth so you know where you need to remove it.

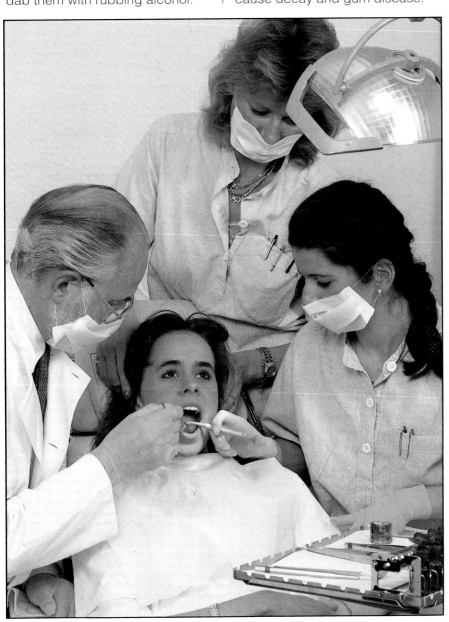

KEEPING CLEAN

As your body changes during your teens, it has to work overtime. You will find that you start to sweat more under the arms and around the genitals. It is important to wash these parts of your body carefully every day.

Underarm perspiration begins to smell if it remains on the body or on clothing. Deodorants stop the smells and antiperspirants stop the wetness. If you decide to use these, you will still need to wash as often. It is also important to wash deodorants off at night so that the pores on your underarm skin get a chance to "breathe" properly and don't get clogged up.

▲ Stale sweat can smell, so it is best to wash frequently under your arms and around your genitals.

▲ Personal hygiene is extremely important at any age, but especially during adolescence. Take care to wash properly.

► Many girls find that lying on their backs, with knees drawn up to the chest and a hot water bottle on the stomach, helps to relieve menstrual cramps.

▼ Having your period does not mean you can't enjoy yourself. Sanitary napkins and tampons enable you to do anything with confidence—from swimming to dancing.

Growing girls

When girls start to menstruate, it becomes important for them to pay attention to personal hygiene. Menstrual blood is perfectly healthy, but once it leaves the body it starts to smell, so it is important to wash the genital area regularly during a period.

To avoid spreading germs from the anus to the vagina, girls should wash their genitals from front to back. Perfumed soap can lead to skin irritations around genitals, so it is better to use only unperfumed soap or water on its own.

However light a girl's blood flow, tampons should be changed after six hours and sanitary napkins after four hours; otherwise, the blood will start to smell. It does no harm to change tampons or napkins as frequently as you like. Vaginal deodorants and sprays should never be used. They contain chemicals that irritate the vagina.

Throughout the month, girls have a slight milky white discharge that has a natural odor. This discharge turns faintly yellowish in color once it leaves the vagina. Discharge that suddenly becomes thicker and lumpy, changes color or smells bad can be a sign of a vaginal infection. The solution is to go to a doctor or clinic: A minor infection left untreated can lead to more serious problems. Most vaginal infections can be easily treated, and the checkup will put your mind at rest.

Another complaint common with girls is cystitis, an infection of the bladder. Ways to prevent or aid recovery from vaginal irritations or cystitis include:

● Using nonbiological washing powder—some of the chemicals in "biological" powders irritate the skin.
● Wearing cotton underpants instead of nylon ones, because anything made of artificial material will make you sweat more. Excessive sweating in the genital area can lead to a spread of infection because the skin cannot "breathe."
● Avoiding clothes that fit tightly around the crotch.

▼ If you decide to wear a bra, measure yourself properly to get one that is comfortable. Remember your size will change as you develop.

▶ If you want to go swimming when you are having your period, you can wear a tampon, which is worn internally.

Measuring for a bra
Some girls like to wear bras as their breasts grow during puberty. Do not feel you must wear a bra if you are comfortable without one. But if you do, you should make sure it fits properly.

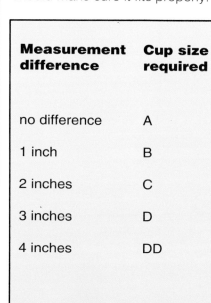

Measurement difference	Cup size required
no difference	A
1 inch	B
2 inches	C
3 inches	D
4 inches	DD

To measure yourself for a bra, first measure around the chest under your breasts and then add five inches. To work out your cup size, measure around the chest again but this time around the fullest part at the nipple. Then take the first measurement away from the second one. The difference is the cup size.

Boys and bodies

Like girls, teenage boys need to pay attention to personal hygiene.

Some boys are circumcised. This means that the foreskin on the penis has been removed in an operation. If you still have a foreskin, you will notice that beneath it, a white, creamy substance called smegma is produced. This helps the skin glide over the tip of your penis. Along with smegma, semen and other fluids can accumulate beneath the foreskin. If you do not wash regularly, these fluids will smell and can lead to infections. It is important to roll back your foreskin and gently wash underneath it daily.

Wet dreams

During adolescence, boys produce a lot of semen and may

▲ Bath time is a time not only for getting clean but for relaxation after a long day.

sometimes have wet dreams. This means when you are asleep, you have an erection and ejaculate semen. This is normal. However, if this worries you, you can keep some tissues by the bed to wipe away any discharge.

If you want to get any stains off the sheets, you can wipe them with a slightly damp cloth, but make sure the sheets have a chance to dry out properly before you put them back on the bed.

BODY CHOICES

Getting used to the physical and emotional changes that adolescence brings can seem difficult at times. Looking after your body is not just about keeping it clean and healthy. It is also about taking care and control about who you decide to allow close to your body and to you. One of the most confusing changes is that you may start to think about relationships and sex.

You can learn to take good care of your developing body by understanding the changes that are happening and how they affect you. As you get older, you will have to face such difficult decisions as what kinds of relationships you want to have with people and whether or not you want the relationships to involve physical contact. These are important issues to think about.

Facts first

The best way to make decisions about your body is to find out a few facts first. It is worth talking to trusted friends and adults about difficult aspects of relationships and sex. You need to remember, however, that the people you ask may not always be right, so check any information they tell you by reading books and pamphlets or by calling a help line.

◀ Who you allow to get close to you and your body is an important issue when you are growing up. You need to make choices about your body without feeling forced or forcing other people into doing things they don't want to do.

▶ Enjoying the company of good friends, and having fun with them, is very important during adolescence.

Contraception

If you are thinking about having sex, you need to think first about using contraceptives to prevent an unwanted pregnancy unless you are about to start a family, which also requires a great deal of thought. Contraception is the responsibility of both partners in a sexual relationship. Whether you are male or female, you have a responsibility to yourself and your partner to use contraception if you want to avoid an unwanted pregnancy. However, you cannot assume that your partner will be prepared, so you need to think about contraceptive options for yourself.

To find out more about methods of contraception, you can ask your doctor or local family-planning clinic. For some addresses of places that can answer some of your questions or supply you with more information, turn to page 31.

Intrauterine device (IUD)

The IUD is a small coil or loop of plastic or copper that is fitted inside the uterus by a doctor. It prevents the egg and sperm from meeting, so fertilization is not possible.

Advantages: It is effective immediately. It does not interfere with lovemaking.

Disadvantages: Periods can become heavier. There is a risk of developing an infection from it. It is not ideal for a young woman who has never been pregnant.

▼ Chatting with a trusted friend, as well as with your partner, about contraception is a good way to sort out your feelings.

▶ Condoms and the pill are both popular forms of contraception, but only the condom gives protection against AIDS.

Methods of contraception
The combined and the mini-pill

The combined pill is taken every day. It causes changes in a woman's hormone balance, which prevent her from being fertile. The mini-pill causes bodily changes that make it difficult for sperm to enter the uterus or for a baby to grow in the uterus .

Advantages: Properly used, it is a reliable contraceptive and does not interfere with lovemaking.

Disadvantages: It has to be taken daily, and the mini-pill must be taken at exactly the same time each day. There can be side effects, and the combined pill is not suitable for diabetics, or for people with high blood pressure or heart disease and/or thrombosis. There can be bleeding at irregular times with the mini-pill.

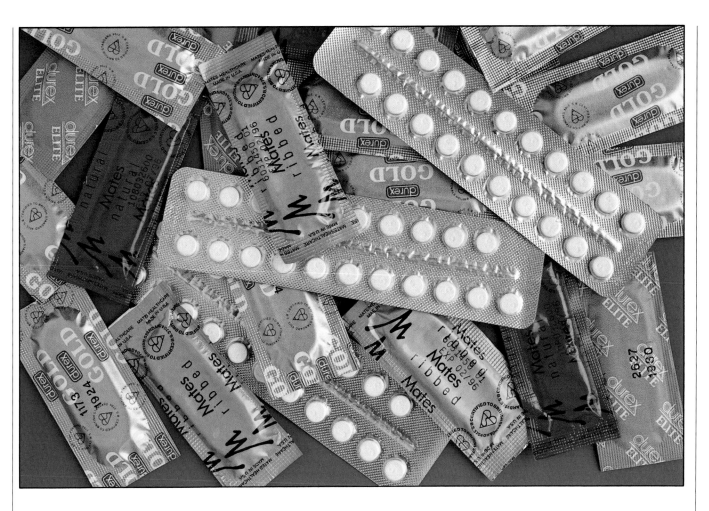

Diaphragm or cap with spermicide

A soft rubber device that the girl puts inside her vagina before intercourse. It covers the entrance to the uterus and prevents the egg and sperm from meeting. The size of the diaphragm must be decided by a doctor.

Advantages: It does not interfere with lovemaking, as it can be put in beforehand.

Disadvantages: Diaphragm and spermicide have to be in place before intercourse, so the girl needs to plan ahead.

Sponge

A soft, foam sponge that contains spermicide. It is placed over the entrance to the uterus and remains effective for 24 hours.

Advantages: No fitting is required, and the sponge can be bought at a drugstore.

Disadvantages: It is not as effective as other methods of contraception. A new sponge has to be inserted after 24 hours. This can be expensive.

The condom

The condom is made of latex and is pulled over the erect penis before the penis enters the girl's vagina.

Advantages: It is the easiest contraceptive to obtain—from drugstores or vending machines. There are no side effects. It offers some protection against sexually transmitted diseases and AIDS. Anyone who is considering having sex and has not sorted out any other method of contraception should carry condoms with them.

Disadvantages: Care has to be taken to make sure it doesn't slip off and that no semen is spilled after ejaculation (coming).

The NORPLANT® SYSTEM

The NORPLANT® SYSTEM is a reversible 5-year contraceptive. It consists of six capsules that are placed under the skin of the woman's upper arm. The capsules work by releasing a synthetic hormone to inhibit ovulation so that eggs will not be produced

regularly. They also thicken cervical mucus, making it difficult for the sperm to reach the egg.
Advantages: Placement of the system usually takes 10–15 minutes with little or no discomfort to the woman.
Disadvantages: The most common side effect is irregular menstrual bleeding. However, both serious and minor side effects may occur.

Natural methods

By keeping very careful records over a period of time, it is possible for a mature woman to work out when she is fertile. Intercourse is then avoided during the fertile times.
Advantages: No mechanical devices or hormones are used.
Disadvantages: This method is only suitable for women whose periods are established and very regular. To record temperature changes and changes in vaginal discharge throughout the month, a woman has to be taught the method by a specially trained teacher.

Pregnancy

No method of contraception is completely reliable. If a couple have a sexual relationship, there is always the possibility that the girl may become pregnant. This is one of several reasons why deciding to make love with someone is a very serious decision.

Facing the facts

It is possible for a girl to get pregnant at any time of the month. If the male withdraws his penis before ejaculating, a girl can still get pregnant. You do not even have to have had intercourse for a girl to get pregnant—if the penis is touching the vagina, some semen may be released even if the male has not ejaculated.

Signs of pregnancy

Here are some symptoms of the early stages of pregnancy:

- A missed, scanty or short period, if your periods are usually regular.
- Wanting to urinate more often than usual.

▶ OPPOSITE PAGE
Bold advertisements such as this one are designed to raise public awareness of the threat of AIDS.

◀ **It is easy to idealize about having a child. However, although it can be very fulfilling, having a child also involves a great deal of hard work and responsibility.**

TAKING CONDOMS ON HOLIDAY WON'T SAVE YOUR LIFE. USING ONE MIGHT.

REMEMBER WHEN YOU GO AWAY AIDS DOESN'T.

- Swollen, tingling breasts and darkened nipples.
- An increase in vaginal discharge.
- Feeling tired a lot.
- Disliking certain foods suddenly or having an odd taste in your mouth.

What to do if you think you are pregnant

Go straight to your doctor or clinic and ask for a pregnancy test. You will need to take a sample of early-morning urine with you in a container. There are do-it-yourself tests available, but it is probably wiser to see your doctor or go to a clinic. If you are pregnant, you will probably want to discuss the situation with somebody.

AIDS

AIDS is the most deadly sexually transmitted disease and at present is incurable. The virus that can cause AIDS, called HIV, is passed on through the blood, semen or vaginal fluids of an infected person. If you want to find out more about AIDS or other sexually transmitted diseases, contact one of the addresses at the back of this book.

Here are some ways to try to protect yourself against AIDS and other sexually transmitted diseases:

- Use latex condoms. They help protect you and your partner against passing on disease.
- Try to keep to one partner.
- If you think you or your partner may have an infection, don't have sex until you know.
- Avoid any sexual activity that involves contact with blood, semen or vaginal fluids.

Safer sex

Looking after your body means protecting it against disease. If you are thinking about having sex with someone or you are already having sex, you need to take precautions against catching or transmitting a sexually transmitted disease.

Many infections can be cured by antibiotics, but it is important that they are treated early on, so don't ignore the symptoms. Unusual itching, a discharge or other feelings of discomfort in the genital area can be signs of an infection. If you think you have an infection, go to a sexually transmitted diseases clinic or see your doctor.

Facing pregnancy

If you are pregnant, you need to face this right away. It may be hard to do so, but it usually is helpful to tell a parent or guardian. If you really don't think you can, then tell another adult whom you trust. Whatever happens, you will need support. You can also get advice from some of the addresses listed at the back of this book.

▲ LEFT
If you suspect you are pregnant, you should take a pregnancy test right away.

▶ OPPOSITE **A close, loving relationship does not have to include sex. It is up to you to decide what you want.**

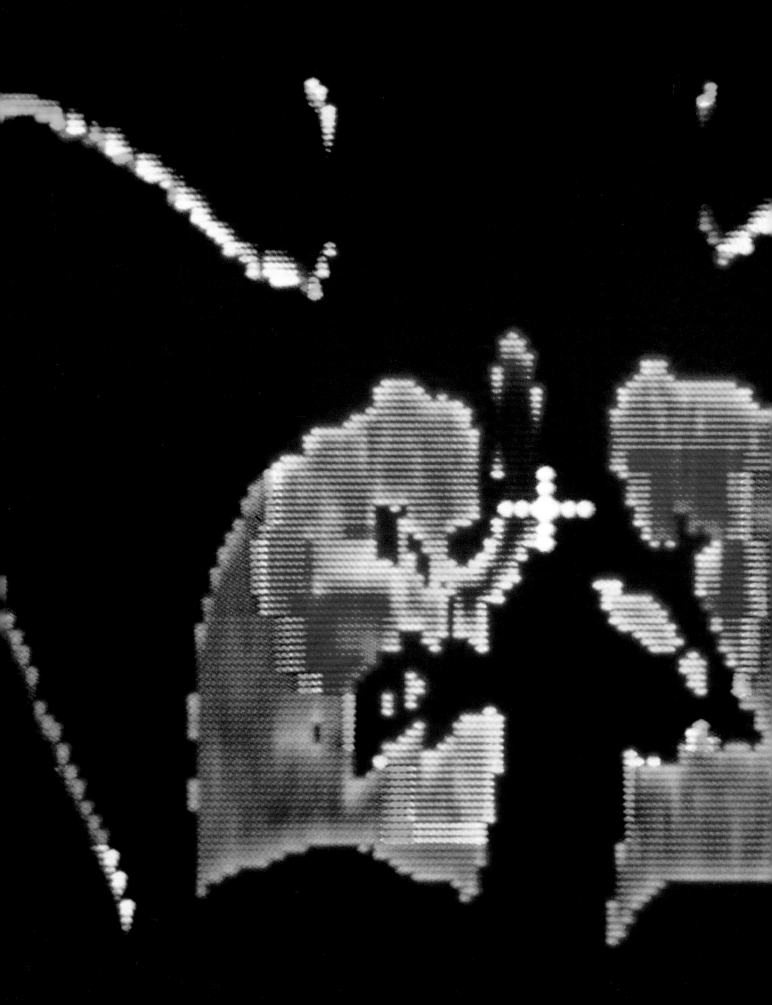

BODY ABUSE

Drugs

Drugs can help or harm our bodies. Different types of drugs have been used for thousands of years for all kinds of purposes. Thinking about what drugs are, and deciding whether or not you want or need to use any of them, is a very important part of deciding how to look after your body.

A drug is a substance that is not a food and that affects your body or your mind in some way. Everyday substances such as tea, coffee and cola drinks usually contain a drug called caffeine. This is a chemical that makes you feel more awake for a short time. When the effect wears off, you are left feeling more tired.

Addiction

One major problem with many drugs is that they are addictive. This means that you feel unable to stop taking a drug because your body or mind, or both, begin to crave it.

Legal drugs

Drug addiction is a problem with legal as well as illegal substances. People can become dependent on medically supplied drugs, such as tranquilizers, which are given to them by doctors to help calm them down. Smoking and alcohol are both legal drugs for adults.

To understand the dangers that are involved in taking drugs, it is

◄ This medical scan of the lungs enables doctors to see what is going on inside the organs. It helps doctors to detect any damage inflicted on the lungs, for example, by smoking.

▶ Smoking not only damages your lungs, it makes your clothes, breath and hair smell unpleasant and stale.

important to find out the facts about what they do. If you ever consider using drugs, you will then be aware of the bad effects as well as the good ones. Look in the back of this book if you want to talk to someone about drugs.

Alcohol
Alcohol is one of the world's most common, legal poisons! It is important to remember that people easily become addicted to this poison.

▶ Many people feel pressured in a social environment to drink and smoke.

How alcohol works
Your liver has to absorb alcohol and make it safe. It can absorb just under one ounce of alcohol an hour. That is the amount of alcohol in just about half a can of beer. If you drink more than this, then the extra alcohol goes into your bloodstream and is pumped around your body until your liver is able to absorb it. When it goes to your brain it makes you feel drunk because it affects your judgment, actions, speech and senses.

If you drink a lot, your liver will get to a point where it can no longer cope with trying to make you sober. This may lead to diseases that can kill you. If you or someone you know has a drinking problem, you need to talk to someone about it. See the addresses to contact in the back of this book.

Smoking—What smoking does to you
Dirt and smoke in the air make the cells that line your nasal air passages produce more mucus. The mucus traps the dirt. Little hairs called cilia push the mucus

▲ People who have given up smoking often regain a greater sense of taste.

Taking an alternative
One way to avoid using drugs is to try to make your life more interesting in ways that do not harm your body. Exercising can be a way of making your body feel good. Or if you feel unhappy, try talking to someone about it, because that will often make you feel better.

up so that you can clear it out, along with the dirt, whenever you blow your nose.

When you inhale cigarette smoke, the cilia cannot work. All the dirt, tar and nicotine cannot be pushed up, and so they slide back down into your lungs. Eventually, the little hairs stop working even when you are not smoking.

The chemicals from the cigarette tar that is left in your lungs can encourage cancer to grow. Smoking can also cause chronic bronchitis, high blood pressure and heart disease.

Other problems include:
- You are more likely to get chest illnesses.
- You are more likely to die at a younger than average age.
- Smoking pollutes the environment for nonsmokers.
- Smoking makes your clothes, hair and breath smell, and you will not be attractive to some nonsmokers.

Stopping smoking

If you already smoke, you are becoming more and more addicted to smoking with every cigarette you light up. The sooner you break the habit, the easier it will be to prevent becoming addicted or to stop your addiction from getting stronger. You can buy aids such as special chewing gum to help you stop smoking but in the end there is no easy way— the desire must come from you.

▶ These people are breathing into a machine that measures lung capacity, or the amount of air that you can breathe in. Smoking drastically reduces lung capacity.

a. A healthy nonsmoker with clean lungs should be able to cope well with aerobic exercise such as running.

b. Because smokers lack oxygen, they have reduced lung capacity, making aerobic exercise difficult.

BODY HELP

Learning to take care of your body means knowing who to contact when you have a problem. Find out for yourself the phone number and office hours of your doctor or clinic. Make sure you have a dentist and arrange to see him or her every six months for a checkup. If you want a certain type of help, such as advice on contraception, sexually transmitted diseases or drugs,

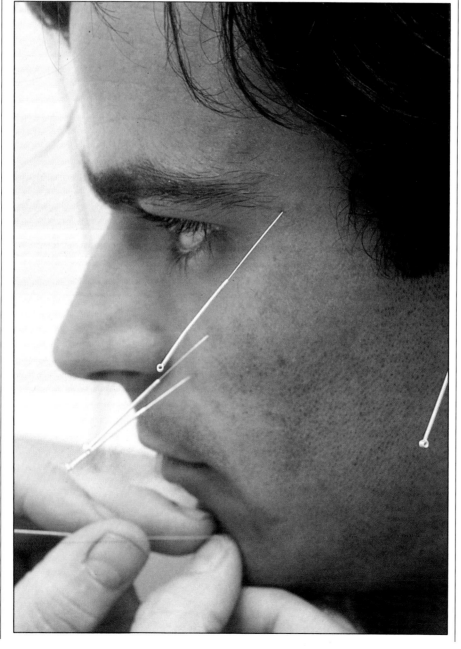

then you need to find out where there is a clinic near your home. To find this type of information, look at the addresses in the back of this book or look in your local phone directory.

You may feel that traditional medical help is not solving your problem. For some illnesses there are alternative types of medicine that some people find helpful.

For instance, acupuncture is a very ancient Chinese way of healing people. It may be worth considering these kinds of treatments if ordinary medicine does not work.

It's your body
If somebody touches you or interferes with you or someone you know in any way that makes you or them feel unhappy, tell an adult you trust about it. If you cannot trust anyone, or you don't want to tell them, call the help line number at the back of this book. Talking to someone who understands will help.

Be nice to your body!
Apart from the points raised in this book, if you want to care for your body, there are many ways in which you can be nice to it. Find out what foods are best for you, get plenty of exercise and try to avoid anything that will harm you and your body. Remember, you only have one body, so be nice to it!

Relaxation and sleep

Learning to relax will help heal your body if you get upset or angry. It is especially useful to learn how to relax so that you sleep well and wake up refreshed. If you feel tense, try studying yoga to help you relax.

Six tips for sound sleep:

- Get some exercise in the evening so your muscles get a chance to relax.
- Have a warm bath.
- Drink some warm milk (calcium, which is found in milk, helps you sleep).
- Read an enjoyable book to relax your mind.
- Make sure you are not going to be too hot or too cold once you get into bed.
- Have a supply of fresh air from a slightly open window.

◀ OPPOSITE PAGE
Acupuncture is used by many people as an alternative form of medicine.

▼ BELOW
Learn to relax your mind and body to help you sleep well.

▲ ABOVE
Yoga is an activity that is designed to allow the body and mind to harmonize.

GLOSSARY

AIDS (Acquired Immune Deficiency Syndrome) A very serious disease that is caused by the human immunodeficiency virus (HIV).

Alcohol A colorless liquid that makes you drunk. It is a part of all alcoholic drinks.

Antibiotics Drugs that destroy or stop infections.

Braces Dental appliances that are attached to the teeth and help to straighten them.

Circumcised When the foreskin that covers the tip of the penis has been cut off. This is common to some cultures and religions.

Contraceptives Things that artificially prevent conception, which means when a male makes a female pregnant.

Dental floss A soft thread that is used for cleaning between teeth.

Ejaculate To eject or discharge from the penis when having an orgasm. This is also called "coming."

Erection When the penis fills with blood and becomes hard and sticks up.

Fertile Able (for women) to become pregnant. For a man, it means being able to make a woman pregnant.

Genitals The external sex organs.

Glands Organs that make chemical substances for the body.

Hormones Substances that are produced by the body and help to control its functions.

Menstrual Connected with menstruation (periods), the monthly cycle of discharging blood that occurs in women from puberty until middle age.

Mucus A slimy, protective substance that forms a layer on the air passages.

Ophthalmologist A medical person who checks and treats eye problems.

Plaque The hard, filmy deposit on the surface of a tooth that causes decay.

Scale A thin piece of dead epidermis shed from the skin.

Semen The thick, whitish mixture of sperm and fluid that comes out of the penis during sexual activity.

Sexual intercourse Normally, insertion of a male's penis into a woman's vagina.

Sexually transmitted disease A disease that is spread by intimate sexual contact.

Spermicide A cream or other substance that helps kill sperm and is used with certain contraceptives.

Vitamins Substances that are found mainly in food. They are vital for the health and growth of our bodies.

Yoga Types of exercise and postures that aim to relax and tone your body.

BOOKS TO READ

Sleep and Dreams, by Alvin Silverstein & Virginia B. Silverstein (Harper-Collins, 1974).

What Happens When You Sleep?, by Joy Richardson (Gareth Stevens Inc., 1986).

Skin, Hair, and Teeth, by Bridget & Neil Ardley (Silver Burdett Press, 1988).

Discovering the Whole You, by Joan Titra (Chateau Thierry, 1991).

Growing Up: Adolescence, Body Changes, and Sex, by R. Gee & S. Meredith (Educational Development Corp., 1986).

You and Your Fitness and Health, by K. Fraser & J. Tatchell (Educational Development Corp., 1986).

The Changing Me, by David Edens (Broadman, 1991).

Teen Pregnancy, by Joanne B. Guernsey (Crestwood House, 1989).

Asking about Sex and Growing Up: A Question and Answer Book for Boys and Girls, by Joanna Cole (Beech Tree Books, 1988).

Diet & Nutrition, by Brian R. Ward (Watts, 1987).

Smoking, by Judith Condon (Watts, 1989).

Drug Questions and Answers, by L. Schwartz (Learning Works, 1989).

Rape, by Joanne B. Guernsey (Crestwood House, 1990).

AIDS, by Mary Turck (Crestwood House, 1988).

information and services on family planning, contraception, and sexually transmitted diseases (including AIDS/HIV). Check your phone book for the location nearest you or call the toll-free number above.

The National AIDS Hotline
800-342-AIDS
800-344-7432 (Spanish)
800-AIDS-TTY/TTD (Hearing Impaired)
Answer questions about AIDS/HIV 24 hours a day, 7 days a week.

Self-Help Center
1600 Dodge Avenue (Ste S-122)
Evanston, IL 60201
800-322-MASH
A clearing house for information on self-help groups. Publishes brochures and pamphlets.

FURTHER INFORMATION

Your local health department can provide you with information/services regarding counseling, family planning, V.D., and crisis situations such as rape. Please check your phone book for the appropriate telephone number for the category concerned. Private non-profit and for-profit institutions may be researched in the same manner.

Al-Anon/Al-Ateen
Family Group Headquarters Inc.
P.O. Box 862
Midtown Station
New York, NY 10018-0862
212-302-7240 (Al-Anon)
800-356-9996 (Al-Ateen)
Information for adults and young

people who have or are affected by someone who has a drinking problem. These organizations can help you wherever you live.

American Lung Association
1740 Broadway
New York, NY 10019
212-315-8700
An organization providing information on smoking and health.

Planned Parenthood Federation of America
810 Seventh Avenue
New York, N.Y. 10019
212-541-7800
800-829-7732 (national)
A national organization providing

National Organization of Adolescent Pregnancy And Parenting
4421A East-West Highway
Bethesda, MD 20814
301-913-0378
An organization that supports and develops programs providing advocacy services at state, local and national levels for pregnant adolescents and school-age parents.

People Aganst Rape
P.O. Box 160
Chicago, IL 60635
800-877-7252
An organization that seeks to teach children how to avoid becoming victims of sexual abuse.

INDEX

acne 6-7
addiction 25, 27
adolescence 6, 15, 17
AIDS 19-21
alternative medicine 28-29
  acupuncture 28, 29
antibiotics 22
antiperspirant 12

body changes 4

circumcision 15
clinics 18, 21, 22, 28
color blindness 10
contraception 18-20, 22, 28
  condom 18-19, 21
  diaphragm 19
  injectable 19
  intrauterine device (IUD) 18
  natural methods 20
  pill, the 18, 20
  sponge 19
cystitis 14

dandruff 8
dental floss 11
dentist 11, 28
deodorants 12
depilatory creams 9
discharge 14, 21-22

ear piercing 11
ejaculation 15, 19
emergency pill 22
exercise 26, 27, 28

family planning clinic 18
fertility 18, 20
fresh fruit 7-8

gum disease 11

hair 8
  body hair 9
  split ends 8-9
head lice 9
HIV 18-21
hormones 9

illegal drugs 25, 28
illness
  bronchitis 27
  diabetes 18
  heart disease 18, 27
  high blood pressure 18, 27
  thrombosis 18

legal drugs 7, 22
  alcohol 25-26
  caffeine 25
  nicotine 27
  tranquilizers 25

menstruation (periods) 13-14,
  18, 20
moisturizers 6-7
muscles 4, 29

ophthalmologist 10

plaque 11
pregnancy 18, 20-22
  tests 21

relaxation 15, 29

safer sex 22
semen 15, 19-21
sexual intercourse 17, 20-22
sexually transmitted diseases
  21-22, 28
skin 6-8
skin cancer 8
smoking 25-27
sun 7-8
sweating 6-7, 12

teeth 11

ultraviolet rays 7-8

vegetables 7-8
Visual Therapy Approach 10
vitamins 7, 10

wet dreams 15

yoga 29

Picture Acknowledgements

J. Allan Cash 7 right, 22, 29; Cephas Picture Library 8 (Peter O'Neill), 25; Chapel Studios 15,18; Chris Fairclough 26; Eye Ubiquitous 6 bottom (Martin Reeves); The Hutchinson Library 13, 17, 21; Science Photo Library 9; Tony Stone 7 bottom (Chris Harvey), 16-17, 23, 26 top (Leonard T. Rhodes); Topham 10; Wayland Picture Library 7 left, 12, 14 bottom, 18; Zefa Picture Library 4 bottom, 4-5, 6 top (Sharp Shooters) bottom, 9 right, 11, 11 top, 14, 20, 24, 27, 33 bottom.